GEORGE,

the DRAGON and the PRINCESS

CHRIS WORMELL

A Tom Maschler Book

Jonathan Cape • London

Far, far away over the high, high mountains,

in an old castle wall, in a tiny, tiny hole . . .

there lived a little mouse called George.

Now George, despite the sign above his hole,

was not dangerous or fierce at all.

In fact, he was rather timid . . .

and clumsy, too!

He was always trapping his tail in
the deckchair.

And he was hopeless at lighting fires.

And if he did get a fire going, he was bound
to burn his cheese on toast.

Poor George was hopeless at most things.

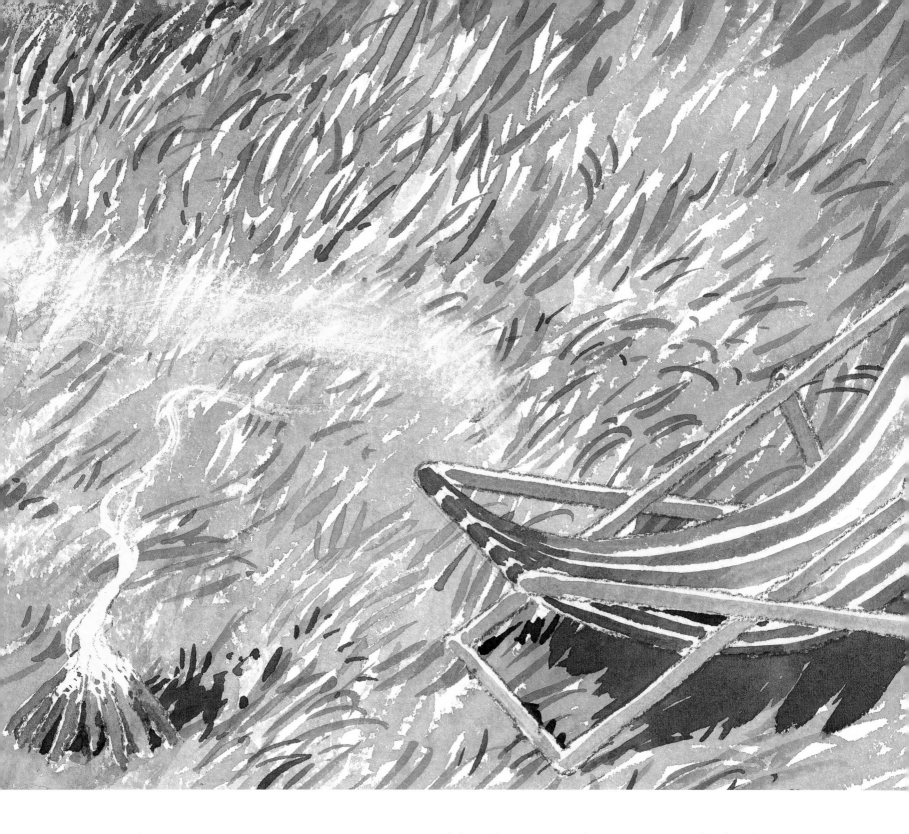

But there was one small thing he *could* do . . .

actually, it was quite a big thing . . .

He could scare dragons!

Well, he could scare *this* dragon.

Because *this* dragon was terrified of mice!

The princess turned out to be brilliant
at making cheese on toast.

She made extra-large portions, so George
could eat as much as he liked . . .

and he did!

To Lucy, Laura and Chantelle

GEORGE, THE DRAGON AND THE PRINCESS
A JONATHAN CAPE BOOK 978 0 224 07072 0

Published in Great Britain by Jonathan Cape,
an imprint of Random House Children's Books

This edition published 2007

1 3 5 7 9 10 8 6 4 2

RANDOM HOUSE CHILDREN'S BOOKS
61-63 Uxbridge Road, London W5 5SA
A division of The Random House Group Ltd

RANDOM HOUSE AUSTRALIA (PTY) LTD
20 Alfred Street, Milsons Point, Sydney,
New South Wales 2061, Australia

RANDOM HOUSE NEW ZEALAND LTD
18 Poland Road, Glenfield, Auckland 10, New Zealand

RANDOM HOUSE (PTY) LTD
Isle of Houghton, Corner Boundary Road & Carse O'Gowrie,
Houghton 2198, South Africa

RANDOM HOUSE INDIA PVT LTD
301 World Trade Tower, Hotel Intercontinental Grand Complex,
Barakhamba Lane, New Delhi 110001, India

THE RANDOM HOUSE GROUP Limited Reg. No. 954009
www.kidsatrandomhouse.co.uk

A CIP catalogue record for this book is available from the British Library.

Printed in Singapore